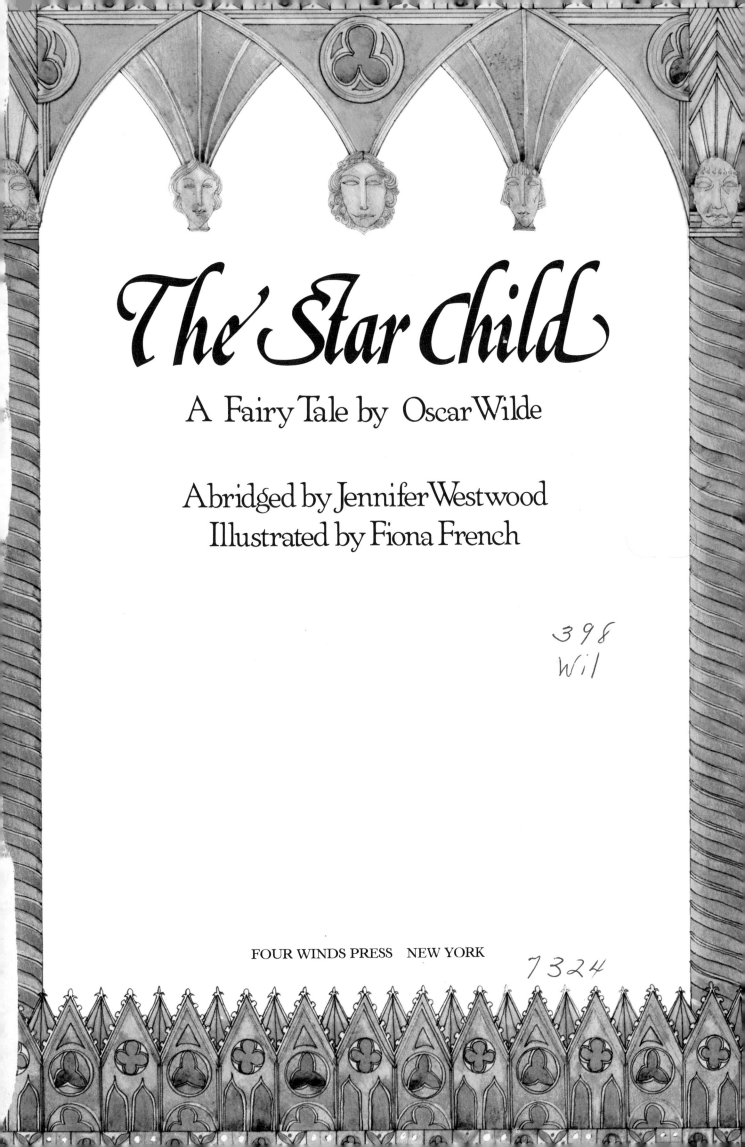

The Star Child

A Fairy Tale by Oscar Wilde

Abridged by Jennifer Westwood
Illustrated by Fiona French

FOUR WINDS PRESS   NEW YORK

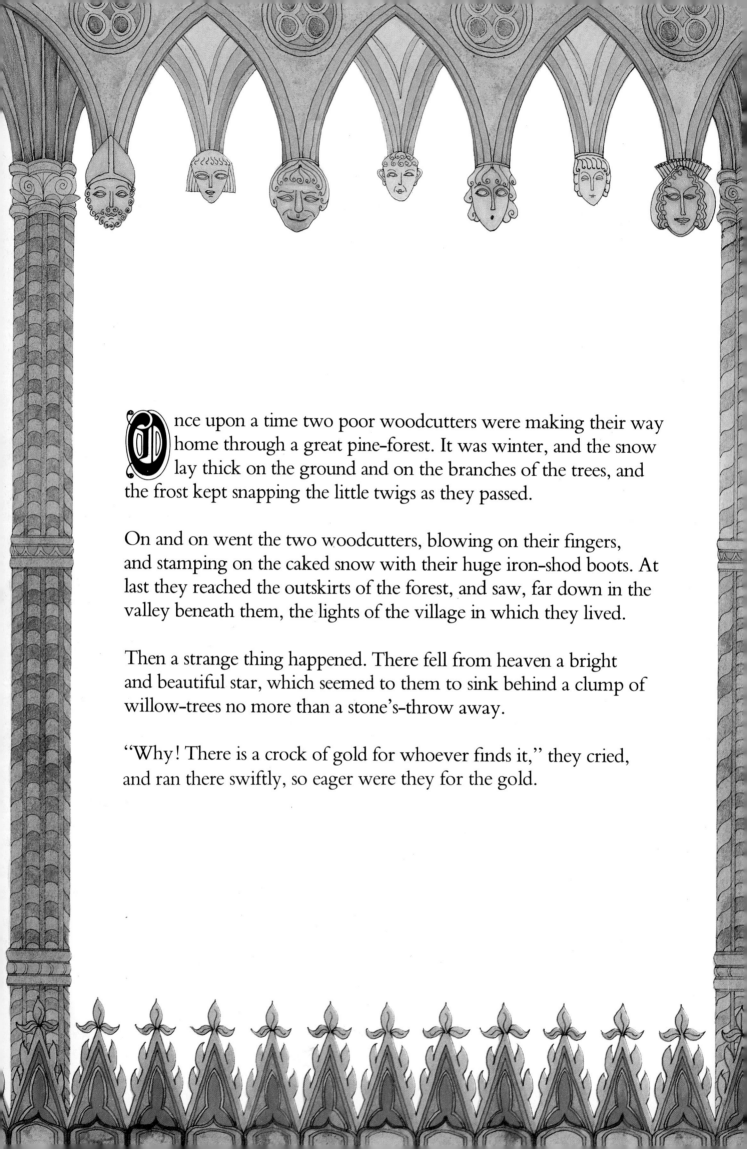

Once upon a time two poor woodcutters were making their way home through a great pine-forest. It was winter, and the snow lay thick on the ground and on the branches of the trees, and the frost kept snapping the little twigs as they passed.

On and on went the two woodcutters, blowing on their fingers, and stamping on the caked snow with their huge iron-shod boots. At last they reached the outskirts of the forest, and saw, far down in the valley beneath them, the lights of the village in which they lived.

Then a strange thing happened. There fell from heaven a bright and beautiful star, which seemed to them to sink behind a clump of willow-trees no more than a stone's-throw away.

"Why! There is a crock of gold for whoever finds it," they cried, and ran there swiftly, so eager were they for the gold.

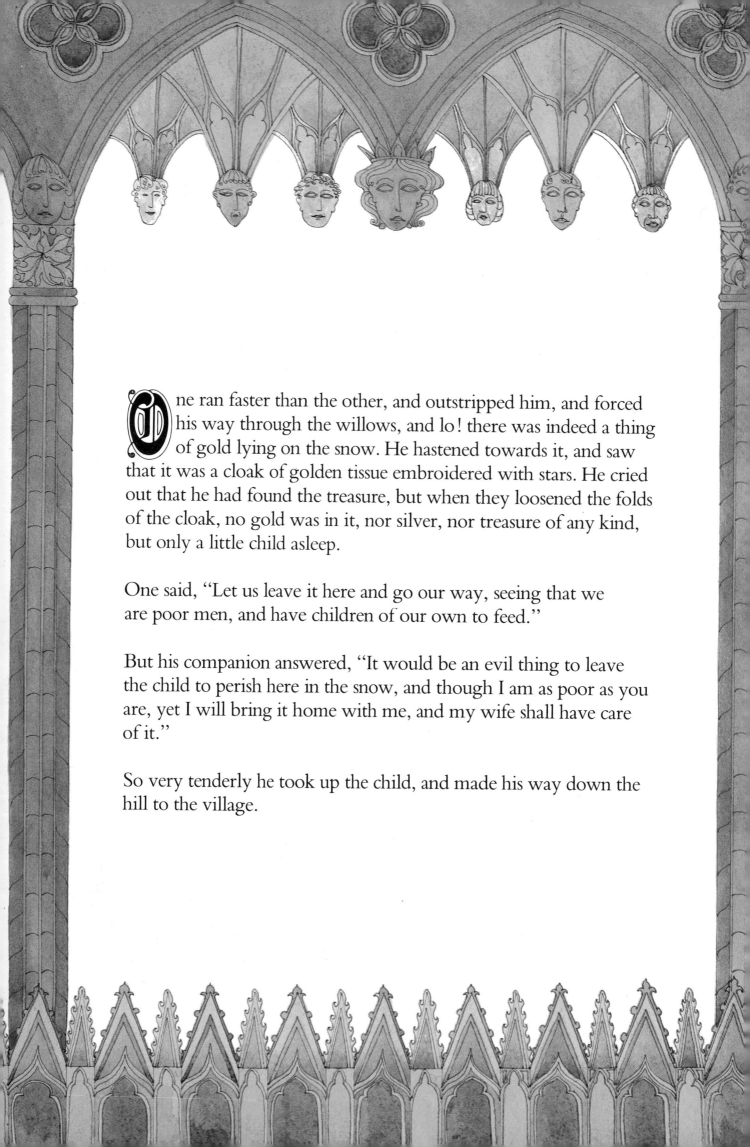

One ran faster than the other, and outstripped him, and forced his way through the willows, and lo! there was indeed a thing of gold lying on the snow. He hastened towards it, and saw that it was a cloak of golden tissue embroidered with stars. He cried out that he had found the treasure, but when they loosened the folds of the cloak, no gold was in it, nor silver, nor treasure of any kind, but only a little child asleep.

One said, "Let us leave it here and go our way, seeing that we are poor men, and have children of our own to feed."

But his companion answered, "It would be an evil thing to leave the child to perish here in the snow, and though I am as poor as you are, yet I will bring it home with me, and my wife shall have care of it."

So very tenderly he took up the child, and made his way down the hill to the village.

So the Star Child was brought up with the children of the woodcutter, and was their playmate. And every year he became more beautiful to look at. Yet his beauty worked him evil, for he grew proud, and cruel, and selfish. The children of the woodcutter, and the other children of the village, he despised, saying that they were of mean parentage, while he was noble, being sprung from a Star, and he made himself master over them.

And wherever the Star Child led them, they followed, and whatever the Star Child bade them do, they did. When he pierced with a sharp reed the dim eyes of the mole, they laughed, and when he cast stones at the leper they laughed also. In all things he ruled them, and they became hard of heart even as he was.

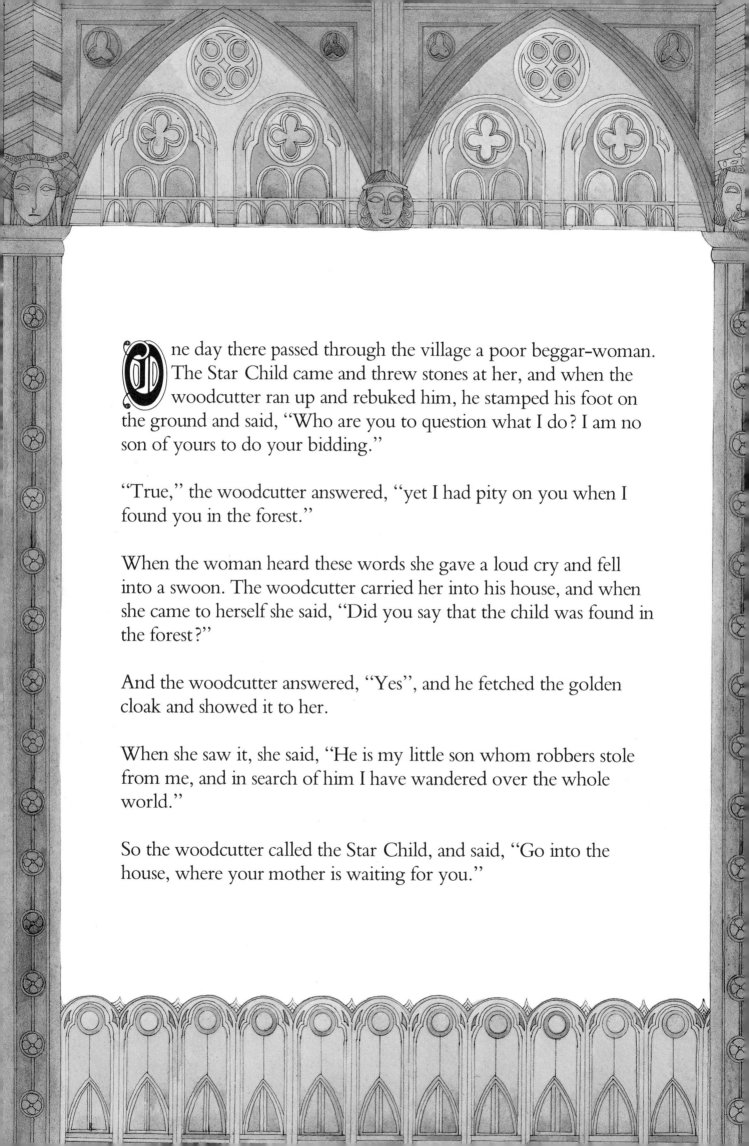

One day there passed through the village a poor beggar-woman. The Star Child came and threw stones at her, and when the woodcutter ran up and rebuked him, he stamped his foot on the ground and said, "Who are you to question what I do? I am no son of yours to do your bidding."

"True," the woodcutter answered, "yet I had pity on you when I found you in the forest."

When the woman heard these words she gave a loud cry and fell into a swoon. The woodcutter carried her into his house, and when she came to herself she said, "Did you say that the child was found in the forest?"

And the woodcutter answered, "Yes", and he fetched the golden cloak and showed it to her.

When she saw it, she said, "He is my little son whom robbers stole from me, and in search of him I have wandered over the whole world."

So the woodcutter called the Star Child, and said, "Go into the house, where your mother is waiting for you."

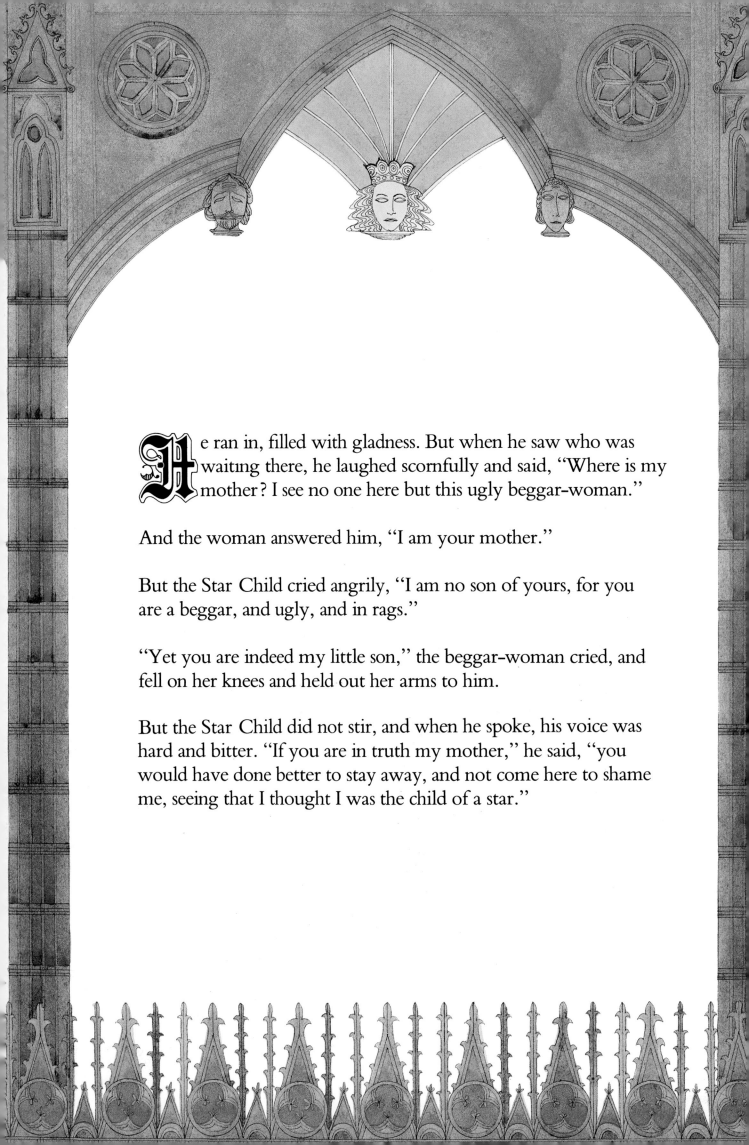

He ran in, filled with gladness. But when he saw who was waiting there, he laughed scornfully and said, "Where is my mother? I see no one here but this ugly beggar-woman."

And the woman answered him, "I am your mother."

But the Star Child cried angrily, "I am no son of yours, for you are a beggar, and ugly, and in rags."

"Yet you are indeed my little son," the beggar-woman cried, and fell on her knees and held out her arms to him.

But the Star Child did not stir, and when he spoke, his voice was hard and bitter. "If you are in truth my mother," he said, "you would have done better to stay away, and not come here to shame me, seeing that I thought I was the child of a star."

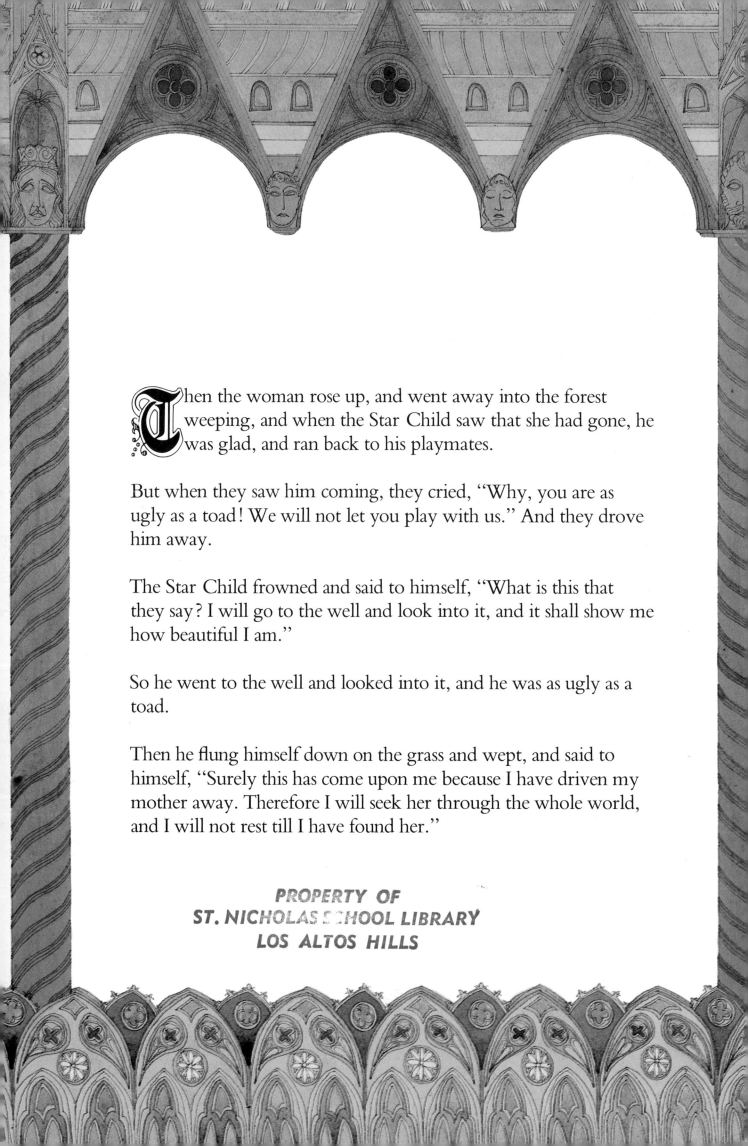

Then the woman rose up, and went away into the forest weeping, and when the Star Child saw that she had gone, he was glad, and ran back to his playmates.

But when they saw him coming, they cried, "Why, you are as ugly as a toad! We will not let you play with us." And they drove him away.

The Star Child frowned and said to himself, "What is this that they say? I will go to the well and look into it, and it shall show me how beautiful I am."

So he went to the well and looked into it, and he was as ugly as a toad.

Then he flung himself down on the grass and wept, and said to himself, "Surely this has come upon me because I have driven my mother away. Therefore I will seek her through the whole world, and I will not rest till I have found her."

So he ran away into the forest and called out to his mother to come to him, but there was no answer. All day long he called to her, and when the sun set he lay down to sleep on a bed of leaves.

And in the morning he rose up, and took his way through the great wood. And on the third day he came to the other side of the forest and went down into the plain, but when he passed through the villages the children threw stones at him, nor could he get news of the beggar-woman, his mother.

For three years he wandered over the world, and often seemed to
see her on the road in front of him, and would call to her, and run
after her till the sharp flints made his feet bleed. But overtake her he
could not.

One evening he came to the gate of a strong-walled city that stood by a river, and made to enter in. But the soldiers who stood on guard dropped their halberds across the way, and said roughly, "What is your business in the city?"

"I am seeking my mother," he said, "a beggar even as I am."

Then they pricked him with their spears, and would not let him enter.

As he turned away weeping, a captain came up and asked who had sought entrance. And the soldiers said, "It is the child of a beggar, and we have driven him away."

"No," he cried, laughing. "We will sell him for a slave. His price shall be the price of a bowl of wine."

And an old and evil-looking man who was passing by called out, "I will buy him for that price." And he took the Star Child by the hand and led him into the city.

nd after they had gone through many streets they came to a
little door that was set in a wall that was covered with a
pomegranate tree. And the old man touched the door with a
ring of jasper and it opened, and they went down five steps
of brass into a garden filled with black poppies and green jars of
burnt clay. Then the old man took from his turban a scarf of figured

silk, and bound the eyes of the Star Child, and drove him in front of
him. And when the scarf was taken off his eyes, the Star Child found
himself in a dungeon that was lit by a lantern of horn. And there the
old man left him, and went out, locking the door behind him and
fastening it with an iron chain.

n the morning, the old man, who was a magician, came in to the Star Child and said, "In a wood near the gate of this city there are three pieces of gold. One is of white gold, and another is of yellow gold, and the gold of the third one is red. Today you must bring me the piece of white gold, and if you bring it not back, I will beat you. Get you gone quickly, and at sunset I will be waiting for you at the door of the garden."

Then he bound the eyes of the Star Child with the scarf of figured silk, and led him through the house, and through the garden of poppies, and up the five steps of brass. And having opened the little door with his ring he set him in the street.

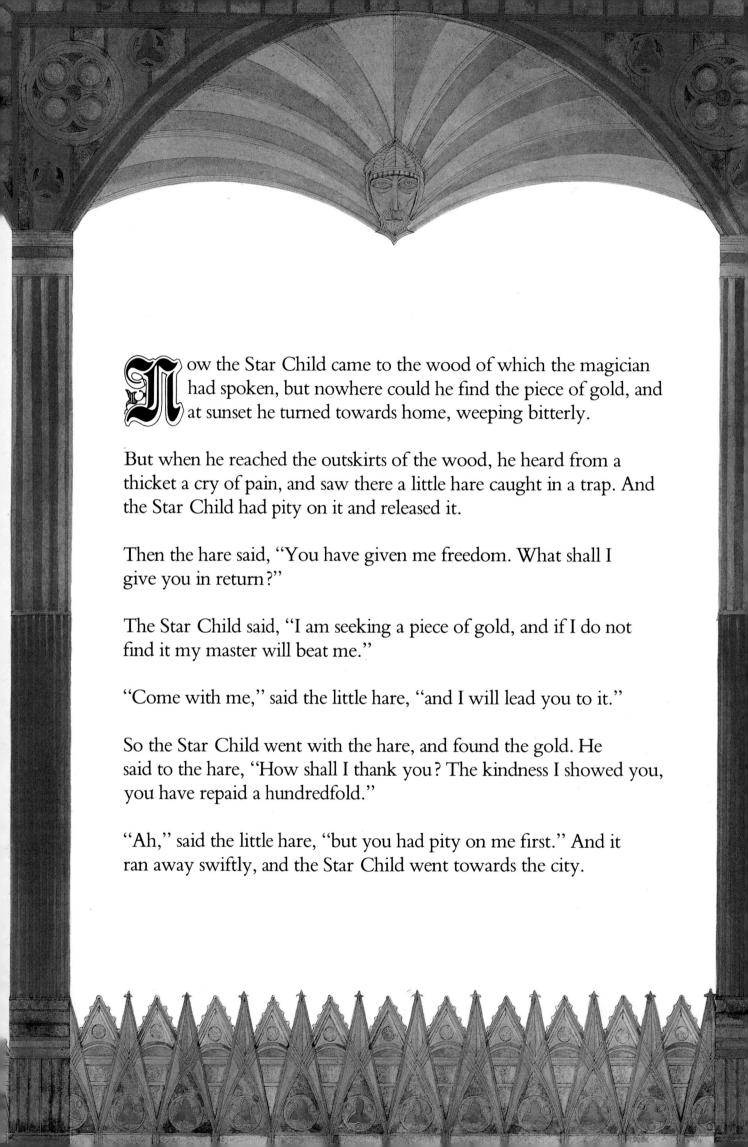

ow the Star Child came to the wood of which the magician had spoken, but nowhere could he find the piece of gold, and at sunset he turned towards home, weeping bitterly.

But when he reached the outskirts of the wood, he heard from a thicket a cry of pain, and saw there a little hare caught in a trap. And the Star Child had pity on it and released it.

Then the hare said, "You have given me freedom. What shall I give you in return?"

The Star Child said, "I am seeking a piece of gold, and if I do not find it my master will beat me."

"Come with me," said the little hare, "and I will lead you to it."

So the Star Child went with the hare, and found the gold. He said to the hare, "How shall I thank you? The kindness I showed you, you have repaid a hundredfold."

"Ah," said the little hare, "but you had pity on me first." And it ran away swiftly, and the Star Child went towards the city.

Now at the gate of the city there was seated a leper, and when he saw the Star Child coming, he clattered his bell, and called out to him, "Give me money or I shall die of hunger, for they have driven me out of the city."

"Alas!" cried the Star Child, "I have only one piece of gold, and if I do not bring it to my master he will beat me."

But the leper entreated him till the Star Child had pity, and gave him the piece of white gold.

And when he came to the magician's house, the magician let him in, and said, "Have you brought the piece of white gold?" And the Star Child said, "I have not." So the magician beat him and flung him again into the dungeon.

And with the yellow gold and the red, it happened as before, that the Star Child found them through the help of the little hare, but the leper begged them from him. And for want of the yellow gold he was beaten, but of the red the magician had promised that, if the Star Child brought it not, he would slay him.

Yet the Star Child had pity on the leper as before, and gave him the piece of red gold, saying, "Your need is greater than mine." But his heart was heavy, for he knew what evil fate awaited him.

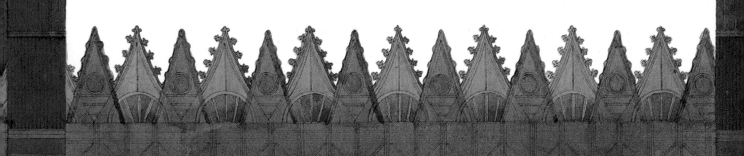

But as he passed through the gate of the city, the guards bowed down before him, saying, "How beautiful is our young lord!" and the high officers of the city came out to meet him, and they knelt down before him and said, "You are the lord for whom we have been waiting, and the son of our King."

And the Star Child answered, "I am no king's son, but the child of a poor beggar-woman. And why do you say that I am beautiful, when I know that I am evil to look at?"

Then the captain who had sold him to the magician held up a shield, and the Star Child looked, and lo! his beauty had come back to him.

But he said to them, "I am not worthy to be your king, for I have denied my mother, and may not rest till I have found her. Therefore, let me go."

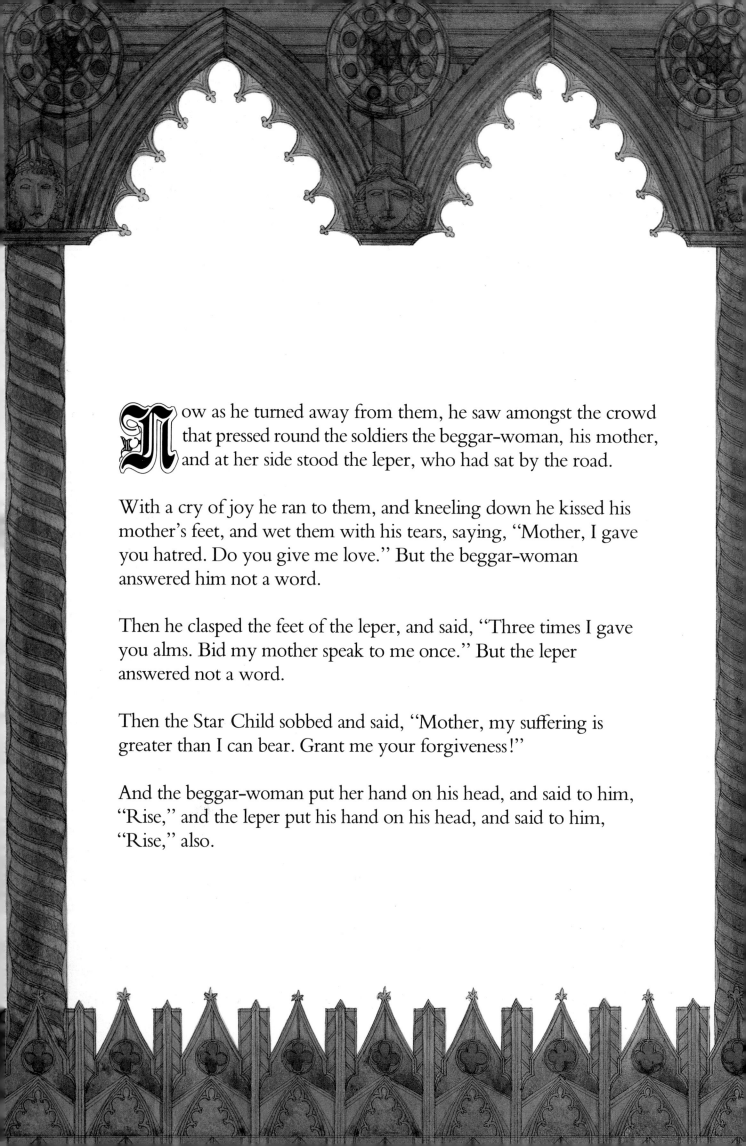

ow as he turned away from them, he saw amongst the crowd that pressed round the soldiers the beggar-woman, his mother, and at her side stood the leper, who had sat by the road.

With a cry of joy he ran to them, and kneeling down he kissed his mother's feet, and wet them with his tears, saying, "Mother, I gave you hatred. Do you give me love." But the beggar-woman answered him not a word.

Then he clasped the feet of the leper, and said, "Three times I gave you alms. Bid my mother speak to me once." But the leper answered not a word.

Then the Star Child sobbed and said, "Mother, my suffering is greater than I can bear. Grant me your forgiveness!"

And the beggar-woman put her hand on his head, and said to him, "Rise," and the leper put his hand on his head, and said to him, "Rise," also.

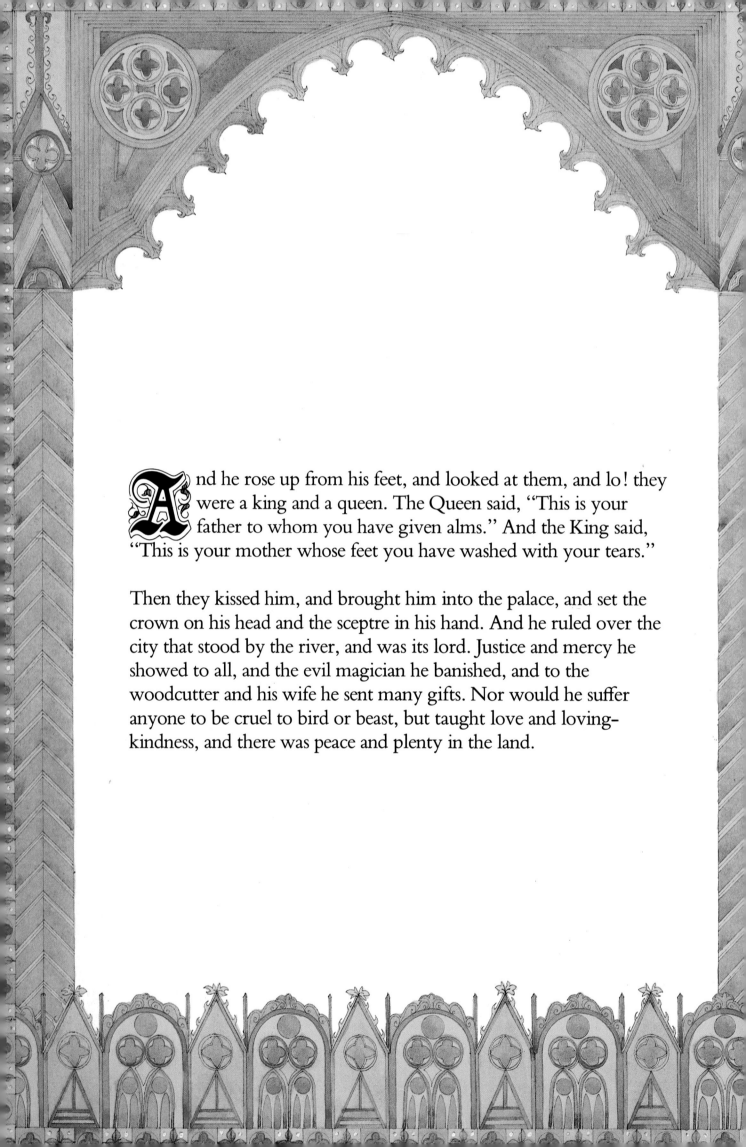

And he rose up from his feet, and looked at them, and lo! they were a king and a queen. The Queen said, "This is your father to whom you have given alms." And the King said, "This is your mother whose feet you have washed with your tears."

Then they kissed him, and brought him into the palace, and set the crown on his head and the sceptre in his hand. And he ruled over the city that stood by the river, and was its lord. Justice and mercy he showed to all, and the evil magician he banished, and to the woodcutter and his wife he sent many gifts. Nor would he suffer anyone to be cruel to bird or beast, but taught love and loving-kindness, and there was peace and plenty in the land.

Published by Four Winds Press
A division of Scholastic Magazines, Inc., New York, N.Y.
First American Edition 1979

Illustrations © 1979 Fiona French
Adaptation © 1979 Jennifer Westwood

First published 1979 by Evans Brothers Limited,
Montague House, Russell Square,
London, WC1B 5BX

ISBN 0-590-07641-8
Library of Congress Catalog Card Number: 79-10564

Printed in Great Britain